DAWN *and the* ROUND TO-IT

DAWN *and the* ROUND TO-IT

by

Irene Smalls

illustrated by

Tyrone Geter

SIMON & SCHUSTER BOOKS FOR YOUNG READERS
Published by Simon & Schuster
New York London Toronto Sydney Tokyo Singapore

jE

SIMON & SCHUSTER BOOKS FOR YOUNG READERS
Simon & Schuster, Rockefeller Center
1230 Avenue of the Americas, New York, New York 10020
Text copyright © 1994 by Irene Smalls
Illustrations copyright © 1994 by Tyrone Geter
SIMON & SCHUSTER BOOKS FOR YOUNG READERS
is a trademark of Simon & Schuster.
Designed by Vicki Kalajian.
The text for this book is set in 16 point Usherwood Medium.
The illustrations were done in acrylic.
Manufactured in the United States of America

10 9 8 7 6 5 4 3 2 1

Library of Congress Cataloging-in-Publication Data
Smalls, Irene. Dawn and the round to-it / by Irene Smalls ;
illustrated by Tyrone Geter.   p.   cm.
Summary: A young girl wants someone to play with her,
but the members of her family are all too busy.
[1. Family life—Fiction. 2. Afro-Americans—Fiction.]
I. Geter, Tyrone, ill.   II. Title.   PZ7.S63915Daw
1993   [E]—dc20   93–19731   CIP
ISBN: 0-671-87166-8

For my daughter
First comes the Dawn,
I love you, Black child
—I.S.

For my wife, Hauwa, and my children,
Gerald, Jamila, and Hafizah. I love you all.
You make me believe.
—T.G.

Dawn always got up early in the morning. Dawn dawning at dawn is what Dawn's mother called it. Dawn at five was round and brown—still round enough to cuddle and brown like the cuddliest bear.

Dawn stretched and she was instantly awake. "Mommy, I want to get up," she called. "Please come and play with me."

"It's too early," her mother pleaded.

"Jimmy! Hazel!" Dawn called to her brother and her sister, but they just wrapped themselves tighter in their covers.

Then Dawn called her father. "Daddy, please come and read to me."

"Go back to bed, Dawnie," Dawn's daddy said in a gruff voice.

Well, Dawn was tired of sleeping, and she didn't want to go back to sleep, so she sat on her bed and sang out:

"*Somebody come and play today,*
somebody come and play.
And sing a song, it won't take long.
Somebody come and play!"

But nobody came. So Dawn sat on her bed, rubbed her nose in her yellow blanket, and sucked her finger all by herself.

Finally, Dawn's mother got up. She had so much to do today.

Dawn said, "Mommy, Mommy, can you play with me?"

"I would like to," Dawn's mother said. "But I'm going to be late. I will play with you when I can get around to it."

And she took Dawn to school, and Dawn did play with the other children in her classroom. But it wasn't Daddy, and it wasn't Mommy, and it wasn't her sister, and it wasn't her brother.

At last it was time for Dawn's daddy to come pick her up. Dawn looked through the school window and saw her daddy. He was dark and handsome, with large, tender hands that could make cookies, clap like thunder, or cradle a book.

When Daddy picked her up, Dawn said, "Daddy, can you read to me?"

And Dawn's daddy said, "I would love to, but I've got to go to a meeting tonight. I will read to you when I can get around to it."

And Dawn's daddy dropped her off at the house and left for his meeting. Dawn's brother and sister were busy watching television.

Dawn asked her sister, "Hazel, can you sing with me?"

And Dawn's sister said, "I would like to, Dawn, but I have to meet my friends at the mall. We'll sing when I can get around to it." And Dawn's sister left.

Then Dawn said to her brother, "Jimmy, can you talk to me, play with me, read to me, sing to me—anything?"

And Dawn's brother said, "Gosh, I have to call my friend Kevin. But maybe after, if I can get around to it."

Then Dawn's mother came home, and there was
no time to talk or play or sing or read. It was time to
go to sleep.

The next day Dawn's mom took Dawn to the baby-
sitter's house. Dawn felt very sad. She went off into
a corner by herself. Her sucking finger didn't taste as
good as it usually did, and even her yellow blanket
didn't make her feel better.

Dawn took a piece of paper and started drawing squiggly lines, scribbly scrabbly lines. She mumbled, "Nobody wants to play with me at my house. They all say they will play with me when they can get around to it."

Dawn started drawing circles. "When they can get around to it, round to, round to it? Round to-it!"

Suddenly, Dawn had a wild idea, a crazy idea. Dawn started to giggle and couldn't stop. She felt as if giggle bubbles were slipping out her ears and tickling out her mouth.

Dawn set to work. This is what Dawn drew.

When her mom picked her up, Dawn was so happy.

"You certainly are a smiley one today," her mom said.

Dawn flashed a marshmallow marmalade smile.

When Dawn got home, she put the things that she had made in her craft box and happily went to bed.

Finally, it was Sunday. Dawn got up early and started to sing out:

"*Somebody come and play today,*
somebody come and play.
And sing a song, it won't take long.
Somebody come and play!"

Nobody came. So Dawn got down off her bed. She went and got her craft box. Dawn took out the four pictures that she had drawn.

Dawn went into her mommy and daddy's room. Dawn gave a picture to her mother, who yawned and said, "That's nice, what is it?"

"It's a round to-it!" Dawn explained. "You always say you will play with me when you get around to it, and now you have one. Now can we play?"

"Oh, my goodness," Dawn's mother said, starting to cry.

Dawn's father said, "From the mouths of babes."

Dawn gave a round to-it to her sister, who snickered, and to her brother, who laughed.

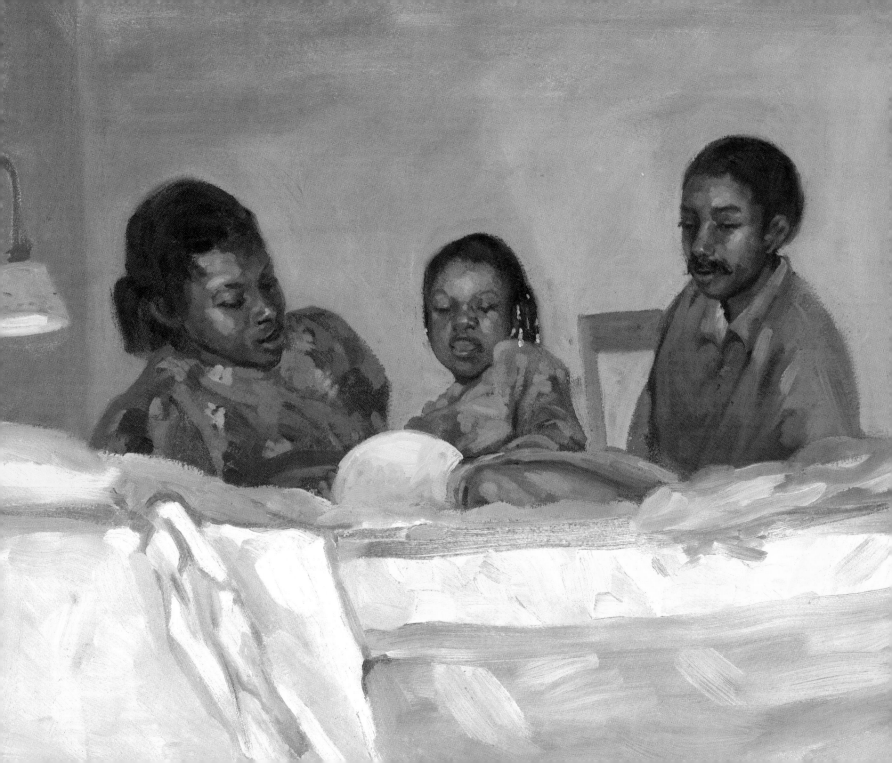

And now when Dawn gets up early in the morning and calls out:

"Somebody come and play today,
somebody come and play.
And sing a song, it won't take long.
Somebody come and play!"

Dawn's mother, her daddy, and sometimes even her sister and brother get up to play with Dawn.

Dawn's mother even wrote a poem about it.

To Dawn at Dawn

I say hello to Dawn at dawn
and she smiles,
eyes wide open to see what she can see.
I say hello to Dawn at dawn,
and she laughs.
Her laughter wakens my sleepy soul
and so I rise.
I say hello to Dawn at dawn,
and I smile at my ebony dawn.